P9-CKB-432

MARSHMALLOW & JORDAN

MARSHMALLOW & JORDAN

ALINA CHAU

:01 First Second
NEW YORK

Good afternoon, Ketut. We are expecting more monsoon rain and thunderstorms throughout the day...

HEY! Watch it!
Sorry!

I'm late...

KMS
11
KMS
15
KMS
23
KMS
7

One more lap,
everyone!
KMS
23

KMS
KMS
21

BAM!!

Wucoatŭ
Cafe

First week of the fall semester

This is how to set up a good shot.
Spread your fingers like this. Make sure there's an air pocket...
...between the base of your palm and the ball...
She's still the best shooter even after the...*accident*.
So awesome!

OKAY! Let's wrap up with a handoff shooting drill.
KMS 5

Gather yourself
Get that elbow in
Aim
Shoot

HALO, J!
HALO, Hans! Come to pick up Lynn?
YUP. Is Coach Prayogo out today?
His baby's sick, so he had to leave early.

GOOD JOB, EVERYONE! Let's call it a day!

That was fun!
TERIMA KASIH!
Thanks for the drill!
Be right back.
See you tomorrow!

Got a smoothie for you.
BYE!
YUM! Please thank Auntie for me!

What are you drinking?

Mom's delicious avocado-chocolate smoothie!

GIMME THAT!

Good try, Lynn!

LITTLE LEAGUE CHAMPIONS
Kahawaii

I'm going to tell Mom you're bullying me!
KMS

LITTLE LEAGUE CHAMPIONS
Kahawaii Multicultural School

Jordan?

I'm okay. It's just...

...sometimes I wish I could play again.

J, I am SO proud of you. Look how much you've accomplished!

Coach would never have let a little kid sub for him—until you!
KMS

You're a b-ball whiz!

THANKS, HANS! I'm not Coach's substitute, though.
Maybe not...but you are just as bossy!
HEY!
HANS!! Just you wait 'til we catch you.

KMS
23

whimper

Who's crying?

HALO?

OH MY!

Are you alone?

Where did you come from?

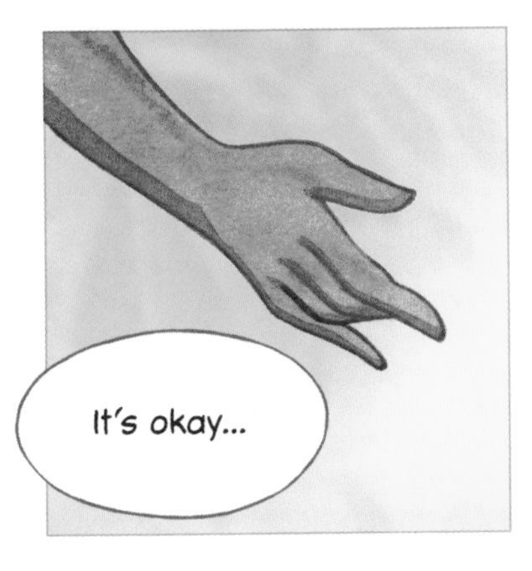
It's okay...

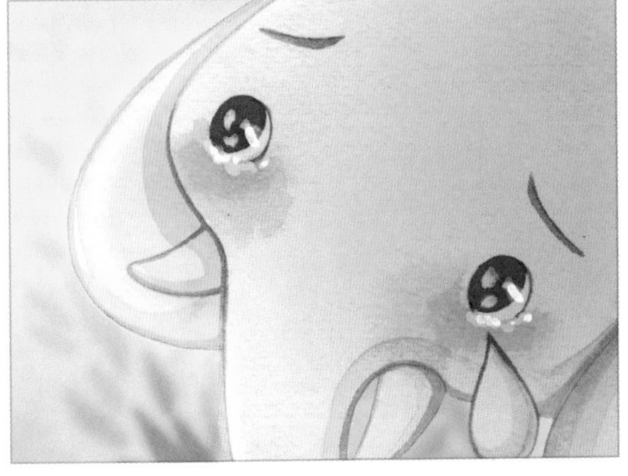

Come here...
I won't hurt you.

Can you show me
what happened?

This must be painful, huh?
KMS

Don't worry. I will
take care of you.

Can you walk?

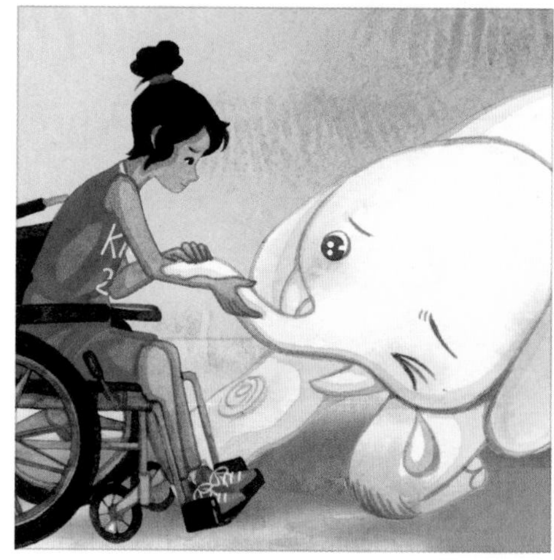

Stay here...

I'll be right back.

KMS
23

This might work.
KMS

Put this under your injured leg.

NOW, try putting your weight on your right leg and wheel around like me.

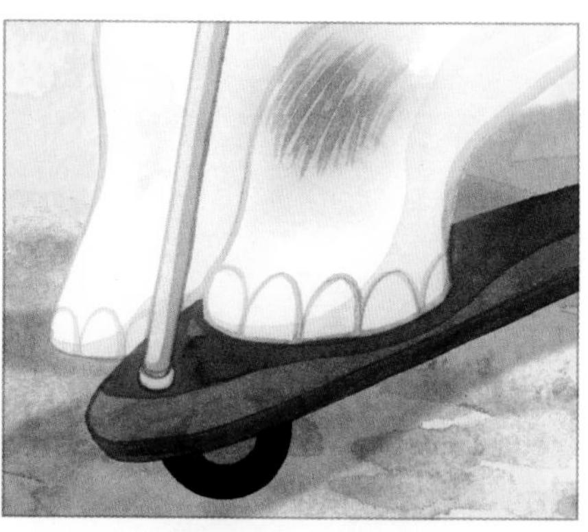

You're welcome.

KMS
23
My mom is a vet. I'm sure she can fix your leg. You can stay with us. We'll have so much fun together!

Welcome to my home!

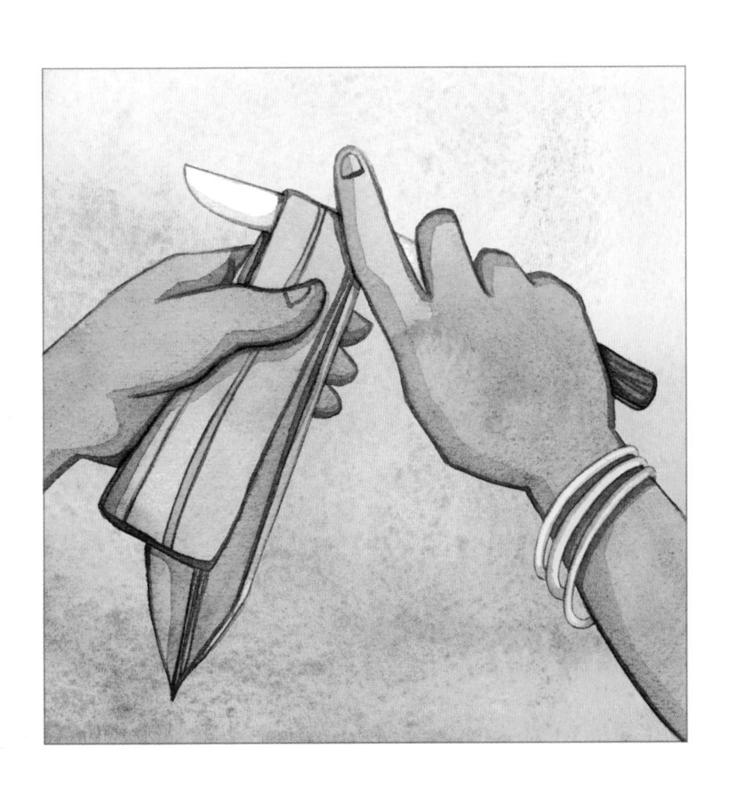

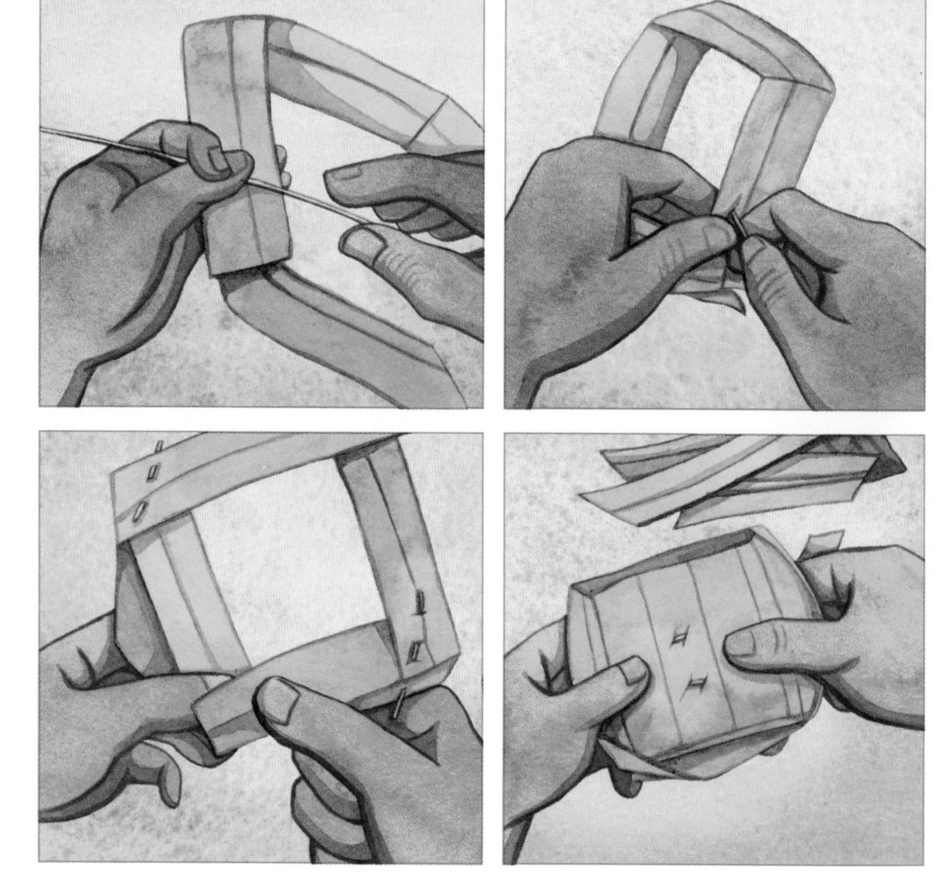

Follow me.
KMS
23

Nenek! Nenek!
I'm home!

How was school,
Onde Dikit?
KMS
23

I made a new friend today!!
And it's an elephant!
KMS

Oh...my!
It's a white...elephant.

Meet my nenek!

He likes you!
What a magnificent creature!

Nenek, can you take
a look at his left leg?
He's injured.

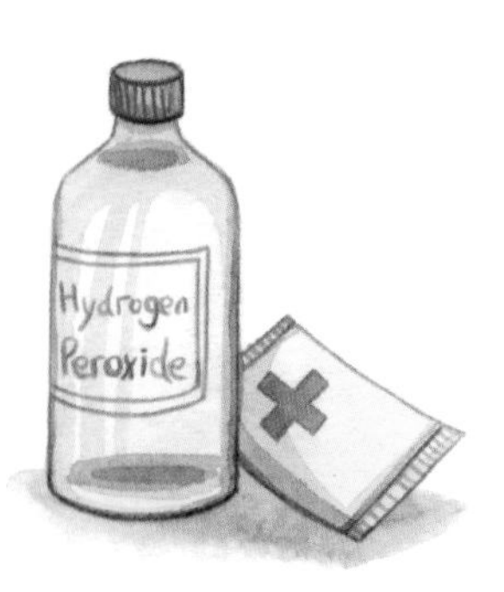
Hydrogen
Peroxide

Is it serious?
I cleaned the wound, but I can't tell.
We will need to wait for your mom to come back to check him out.

Wait a moment... I have something that will make you feel better.
KMS
23

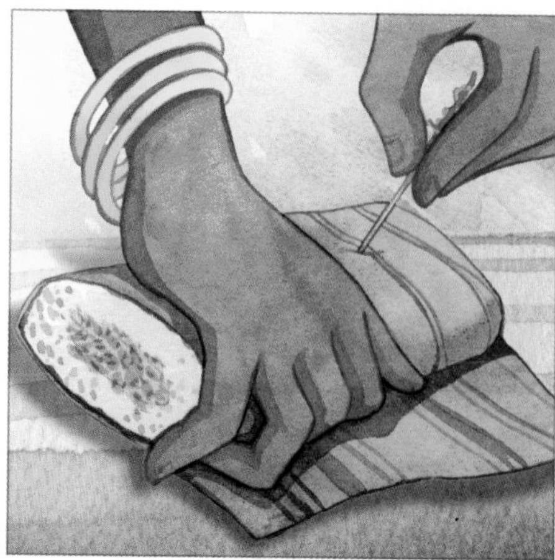

A snack will help cheer you up.
Yum!!

These are fresh from our garden.

Now tell me, how did you meet?

I heard something near the playground...

Terima kasih!
Thanks for the ride!
Don't mention it!
You saved my
calf and cow!

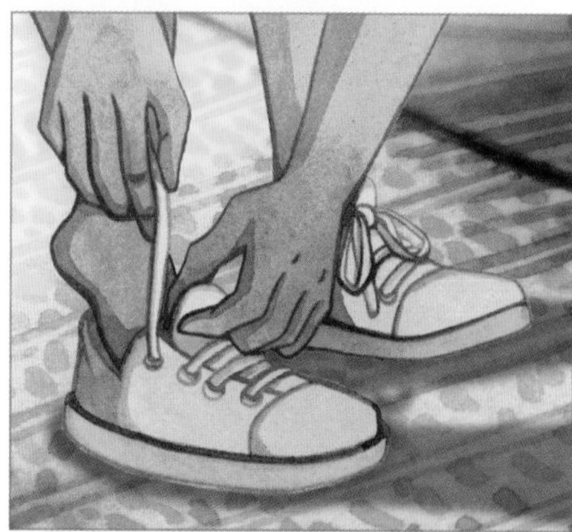

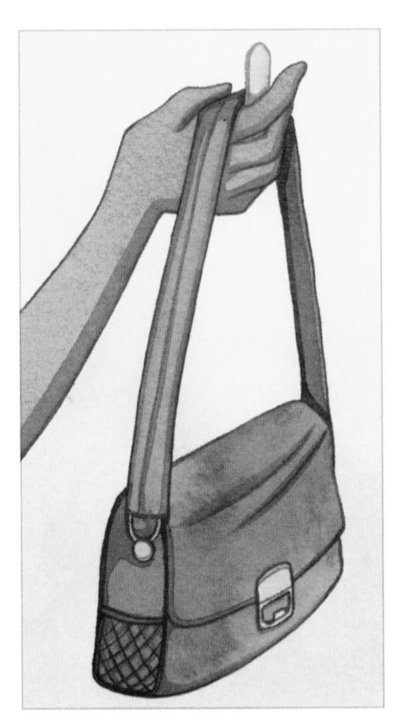

I'm home.
KMS

Hi, Mom!
KMS

AHHHHH!!!

It's an elephant! Why is there an elephant in the house? It's eating off the table too! That's so...so unsanitary. What's going on?! Jordan? Ma?
I found the elephant at the playground. He's injured. Can you check him out?
Please?
KN
23

You must be tired.
Have some guava juice.
And a lemper.
KMS

Did the elephant
just eat a lemper?

Do not worry so much.
KMS
It's eating the offering flowers too?

Ma...an elephant is not supposed to eat meat. It'll get sick.
It's okay.

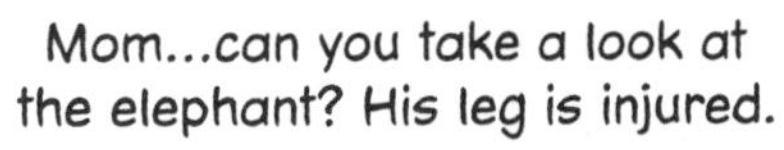
Mom...can you take a look at the elephant? His leg is injured.

KMS
23

KMS
23

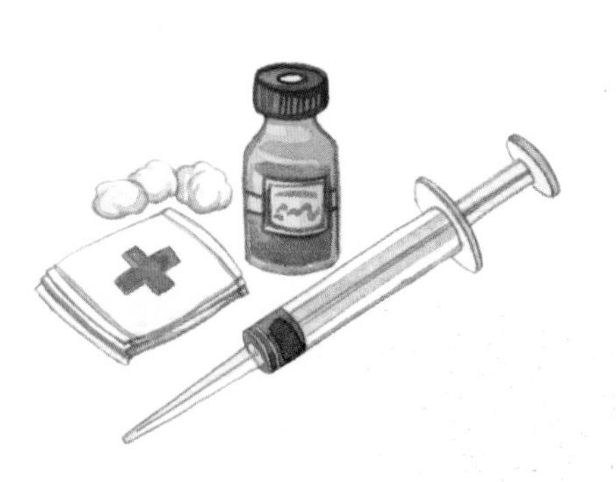

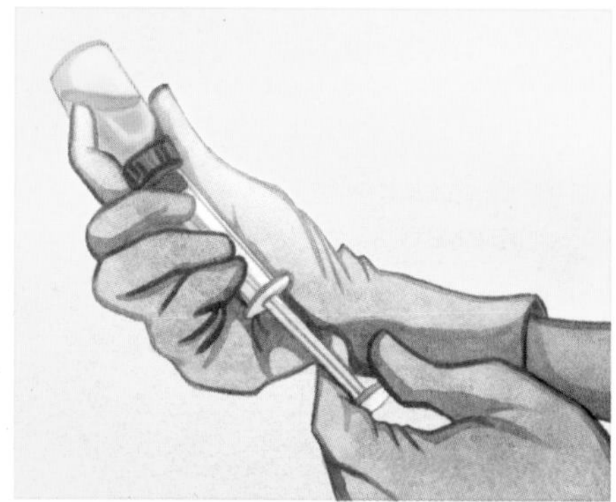

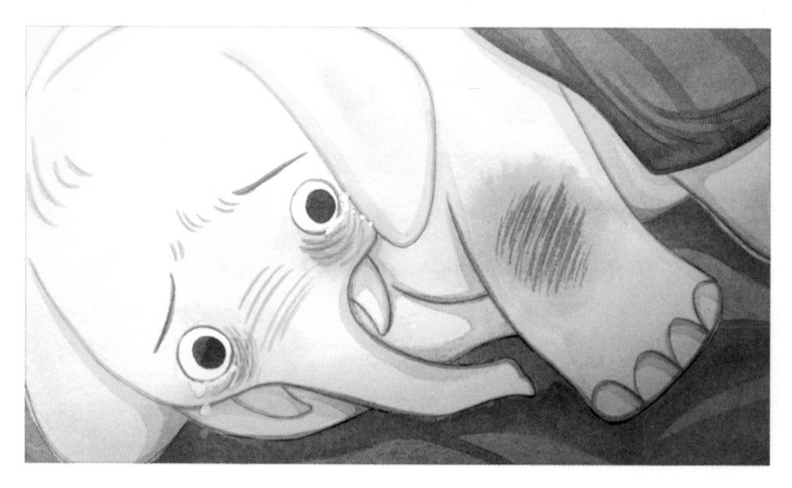

Shhhhh, I'll stay right here with you.

Mom, how bad is his wound?
It's pretty deep.

Can you fix him?

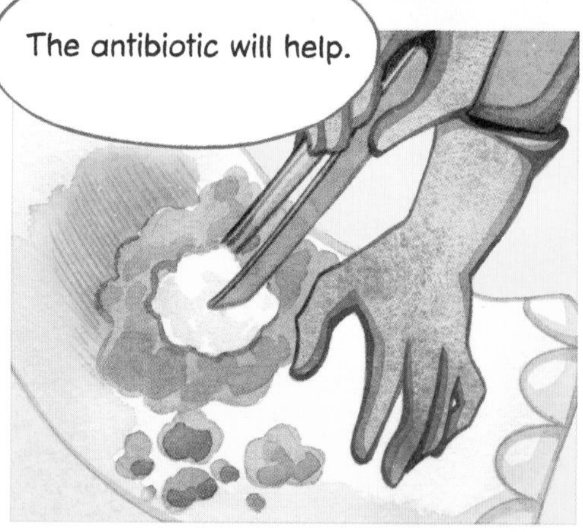
The antibiotic will help.

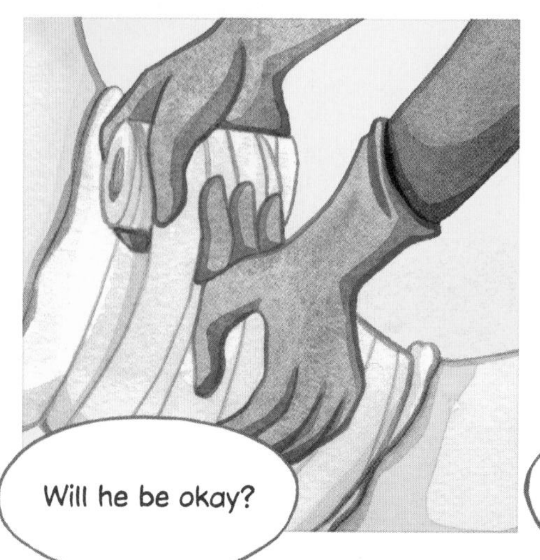
Will he be okay?

Yes. We just need to make sure the wound doesn't get infected.

I mean, will...
will he be able to walk normally,
without the scooter?
It'll take a while for him to
recover, but in a few weeks
he'll be walking just fine.
That's good.
Why don't you
take a break and go
freshen up?
I want to stay.
If you are tired, you cannot
take care of others. Nenek
will keep him company.
KMC
23

Don't worry.
Nenek and I will check
on the elephant.
KMS
22

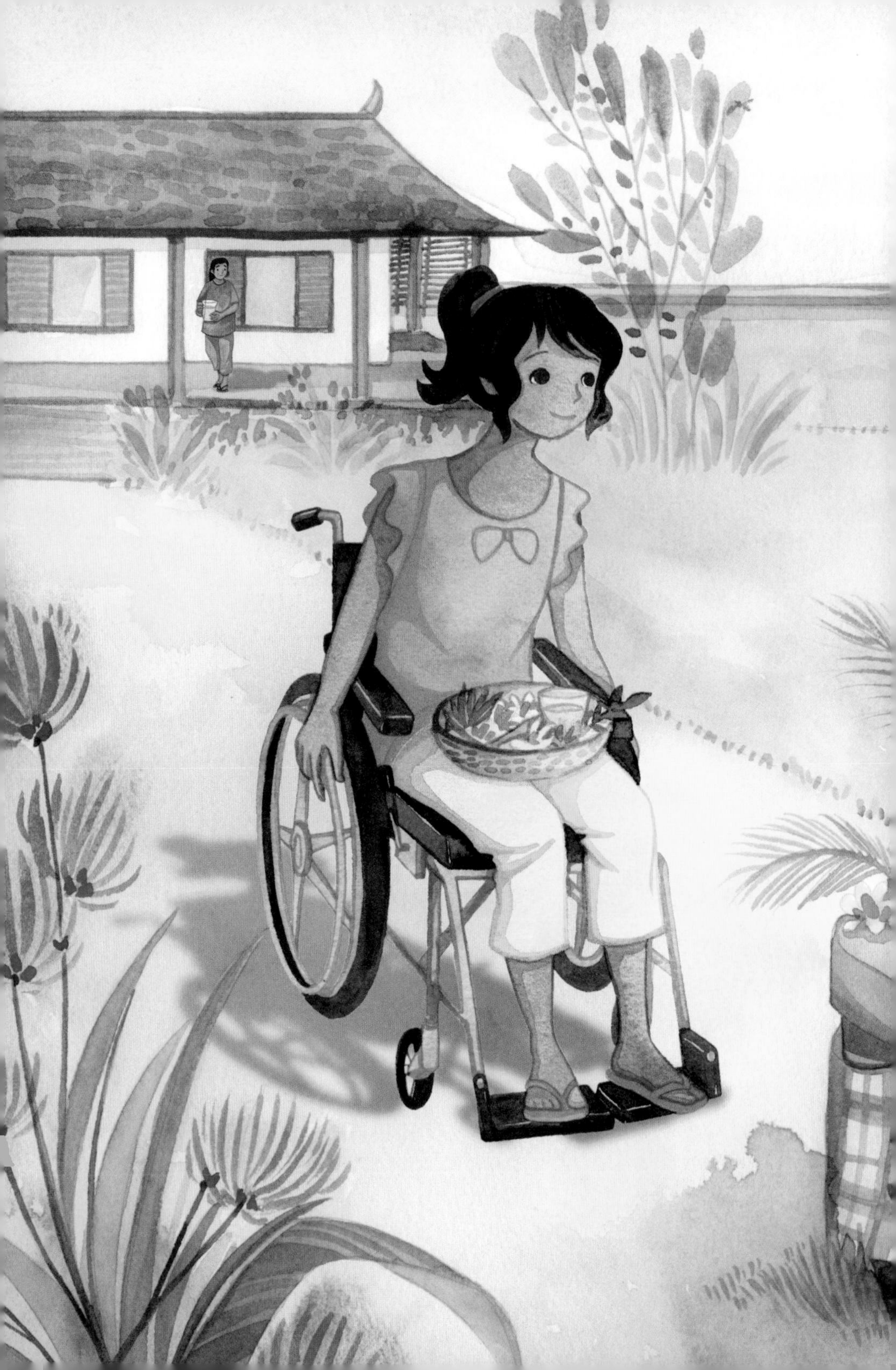

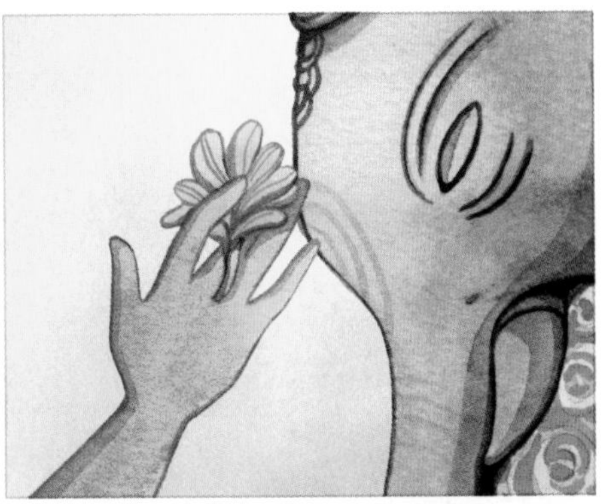

Lord Ganesh,
please watch over the elephant.
Please help him heal.

How are you feeling?

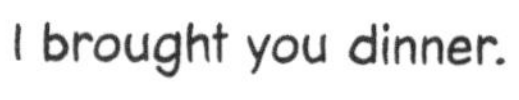
I brought you dinner.

Eat up!

You weren't kidding when you said there is an elephant in the house! This is really COOL.

Now that you are staying with us... I can't keep calling you ELEPHANT.

You will need a NAME.
Are we keeping him?
We can't.

You're white
and fluffy.
The elephant could
have run away from
the sanctuary or a
temple somewhere.

Do you like Cotton Puff?
Nooo...
How about...

Yum!
Hmmm...
How about Marshmallow?

OH! AH-HA!! You like Marshmallow!
Marshmallow! Stop trying to steal my food!!
Let's check whether there's a missing elephant before we decide.
The child prayed to Lord Ganesh for the elephant. I overheard her.

Onde Dikit never asks the gods for anything for herself. What if Ganesh answered her prayer? Marshmallow stays!

THANK YOU, NENEK. YOU ROCK! Mom, Dad! You know I can hear everything from here, right?
You're no help!

Sweetie, you have to admit they are very cute together.
Guess we can keep Marshmallow 'til we find out where he comes from. I'll call Dr. Hartono at the sanctuary.
He could be an escapee from one of those tourist traps too. We may have just rescued a poor animal.
Hehe! You just want to keep him!

RING!!

Good morning, class.

Good morning, Mr. Al-Samarrai.

Open your book to page thirty-two. Today we are going to explore the Pacific Ring of Fire. The geography of Indonesia is dominated by volcanoes that are formed due to movement within the subduction zones between several tectonic plates, including the Eurasian and the Indo-Australian...

...About 90% of the world's earthquakes and 81% of the world's largest earthquakes occur along the Ring of Fire...

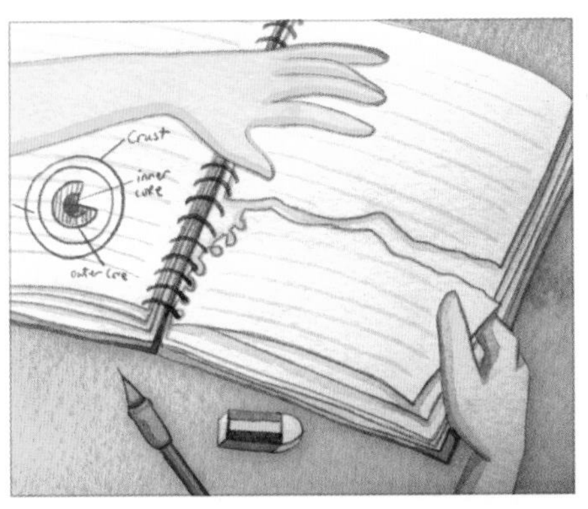
Crust
inner core
outer core

What's going on?
never Late

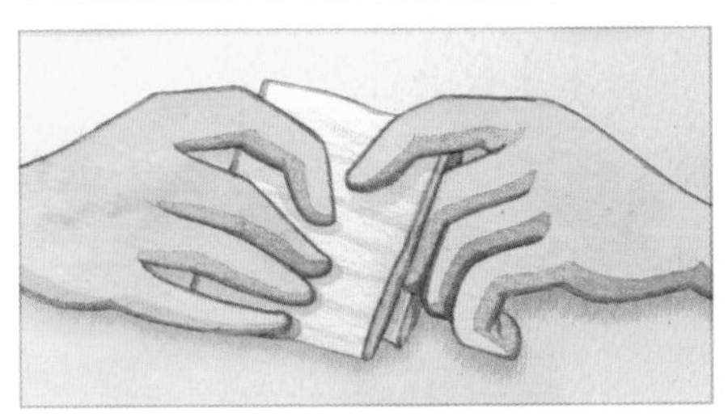

Sunda St

To J.

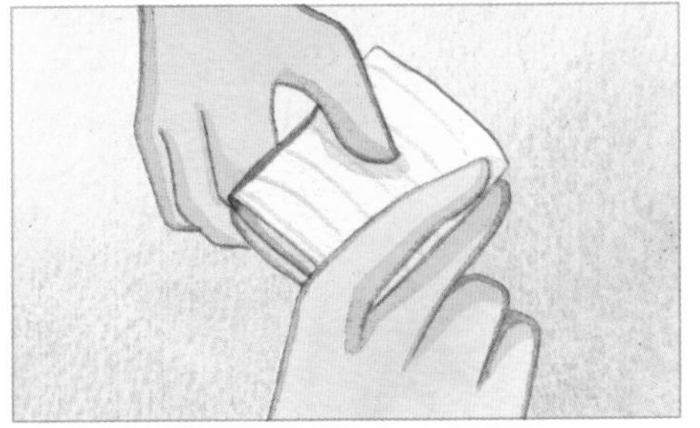

This is the result of the movement and collisions of lithospheric plates.
Sunda S
Krak

Psssst!

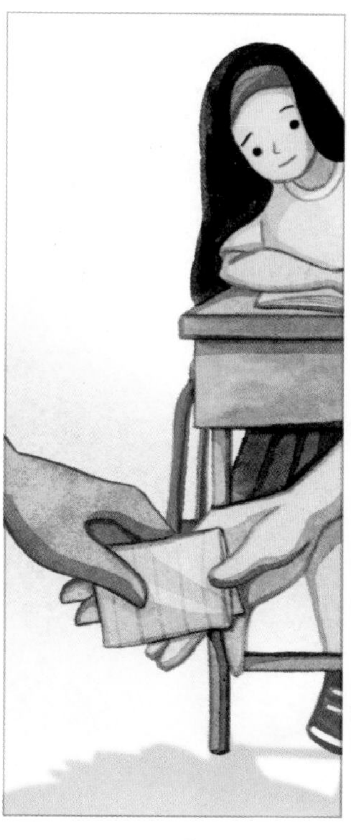

What's going on?
U never late to class. -L

JORDAN! What are the two most active volcanoes on Java?
Krakata

Errrr...

Kelud and Merapi.
It's Halmahera... and uh...

WRONG! Those are not volcanoes.
JORDAN, please pay attention in class.
NO daydreaming.
Sunda

HE! HE! HEE!! HE!!
HEE! HE! HEE!! HE!!
Sorry...
LYNN.
Do you know the answer?
It's Kelud and Merapi.

Correct. But no passing notes in class.
Yes, sir.
Zzz...
KNOCK
KNOCK!!
Isn't it too early to fall asleep in class?!
HA!! HA!! HA!!
Sorry, Mr. Al-Samarrai. I stayed up late playing *Star Wars: Battlefront* last night. It was awesome!

Curry, satay, and tapioca, please.

What's up? You've been acting funny today!
You're never, ever late to class!
I have? Really?

Daydreaming in class
and giggling to yourself...
Spill it! What's going on?
...
OMG
It's a boy, isn't it?
WHAT?!
I saw you secretly
smiling to yourself.
ADMIT IT!
YOU HAVE A
BOYFRIEND!!!
Nooo...
I'm so HAPPY
for you!!

J! You have a BOYFRIEND?!
Who is it?!
Where did you two come from?
It's not what you think...
Is it the captain of the soccer team? What's his name?
How did you manage to hide this big news from all of us?
Are you dating Paul Ludwig?
I always suspected he liked you!

Noooo! It's not what you think! Okay, okay, I'll tell you.
It's NOT a boy...
I adopted a baby elephant!

....
HA! HA! HA!!
That's such a lame cover-up!
We totally get it. You need "private time" with your "friend" who's...an ELEPHANT.

Sham

I heard the big news! Congrats, girl!
KMS 17
KMS 18
KMS 7
KMS 2

Huh? What for?

Paul has had a thing for you since forever. So happy for you two! It's about time!

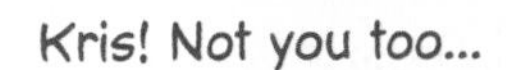
Kris! Not you too...

Come on! Seriously, it's an elephant, not a boy.

J, if Paul ever makes you cry for any reason, we've got your back!

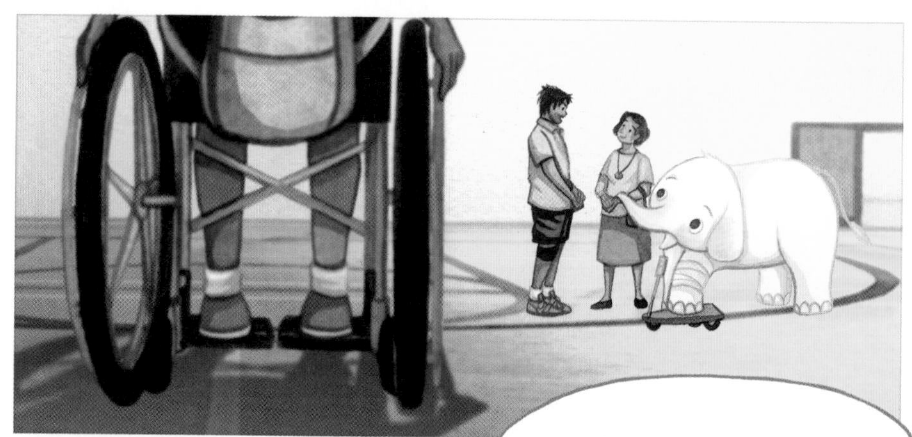

Marshmallow?! Nenek?

Oh good, you're here, Jordan!

No joke!
It's an elephant!!
AWWW...
SO KAWAII!!!

Sooo soft...

Nenek, is everything okay at home?
Marshmallow has been whining since you left for school, so I brought him with me to pick you up.
He is very attached to you, Onde Dikit.

Oooh! You're like a giant puppy! You love belly rubs!
Good job, J! Marshmallow is MUCH cooler than a boyfriend! You SCORED!!

Coach, could Marshmallow join the team? He could be our mascot!
Please???

That's a great idea, but it's not up to me to make that decision. We have to ask Jordan and Marshmallow how they feel about it.

That would be awesome! I'm sure Marshmallow would love to join the team!

Welcome to the team, Marshmallow!!
YAY!!
YAY!!
YAY!!

Now that you're on the basketball team, let me teach you about the game.

Gianyar Basketball Competition
Jordan Winarta

Let's start with this poster of Michael Jordan. He's a LEGEND!

He's retired now. He's older than Dad, but not as old as Nenek.

He was awesome, and he was Dad's favorite.

That's why he named me Jordan.

And that's Stephen Curry. He plays for the Golden State Warriors. He's their best shooter, in my book.
Most NBA shooters are accurate and efficient and have good range, but no one's as good as Steph Curry!
Stephen
CURRY

Steph's speed and consistency, combined with his incredible quick release, give him the advantage...

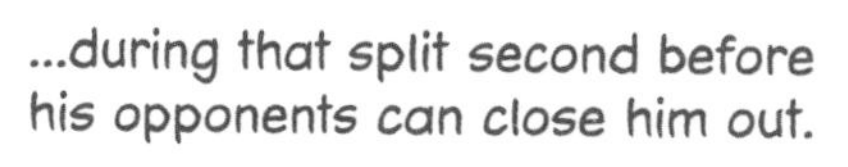
...during that split second before his opponents can close him out.

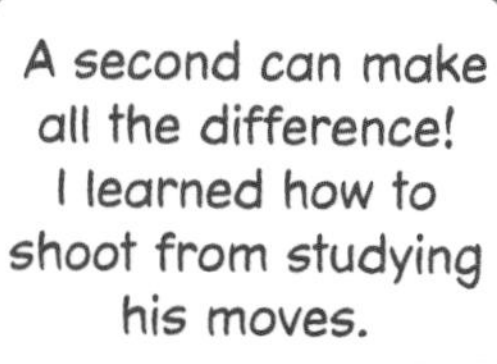
A second can make all the difference! I learned how to shoot from studying his moves.

I dreamed I'd be like him when I grew up... But that was before the accident.

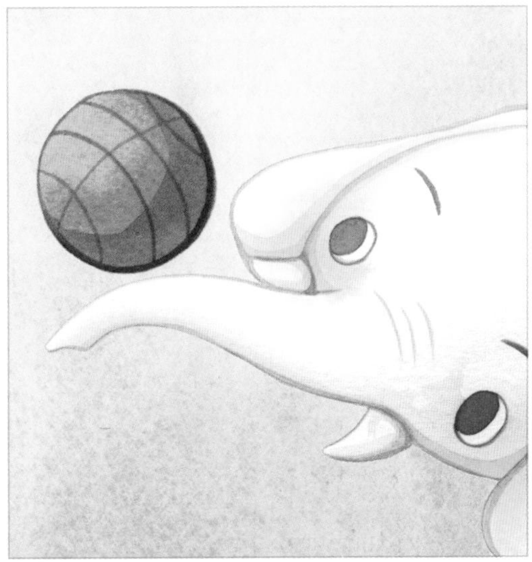

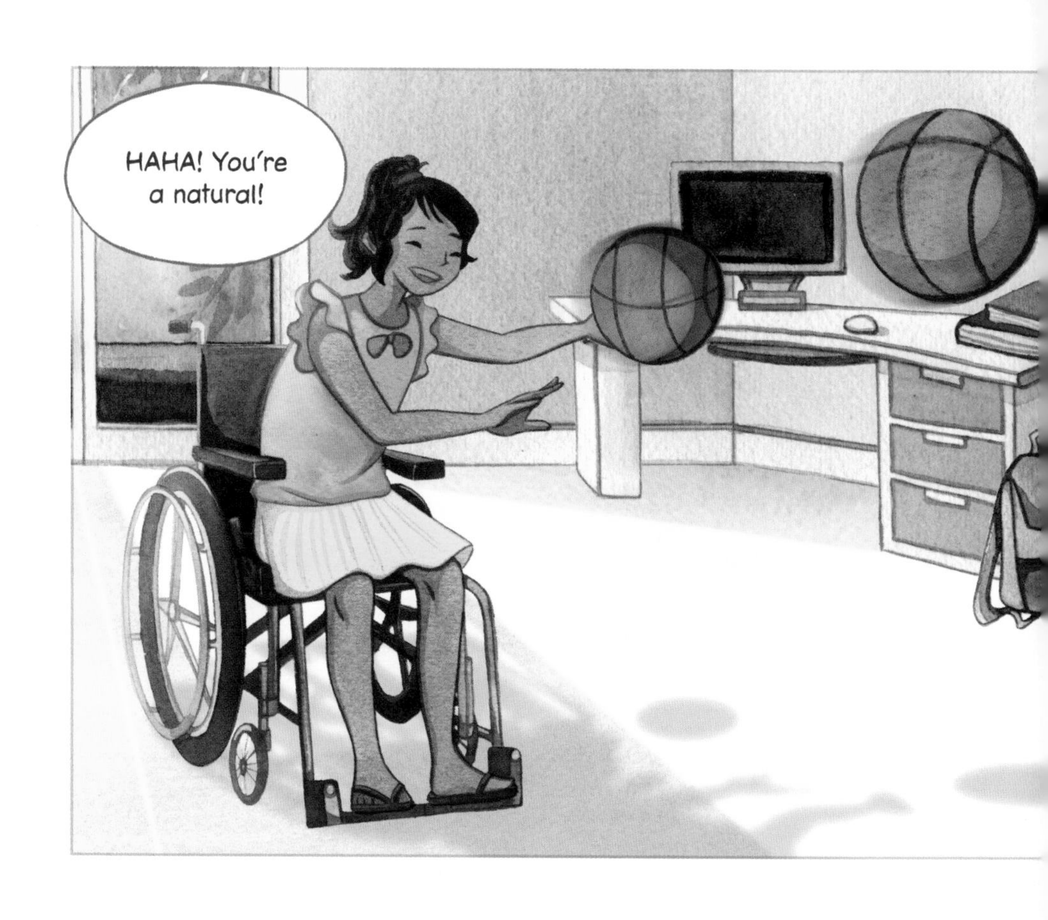
HAHA! You're a natural!

RRY

So cute! She's teaching Marshmallow how to play basketball.

Well, I think Marshmallow will be staying with us for a while.
Really?

I talked to Dr. Hartono today. Marshmallow is not from the sanctuary.
YES!

I could have told you that.
Terima kasih!

A few weeks later
KMS
22

KMS
23

Lynn!

Team Lynn
finally scores
one point!

Chloe!
KMS 17
Hey, Dea! How's the game looking?
It's even right now, but I think Team Marshmallow will win.
KMS

NO!

GO, MARSHMALLOW, GO!

PASS THE
BALL TO
JORDAN!!

KMS
17

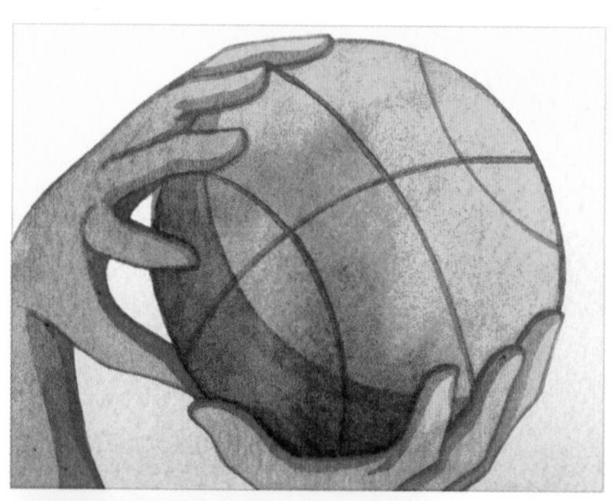

KMS

Time's up!
Final score: two to one. Team Marshmallow wins! Yay!!

That was an awesome game!
You rock, Marshmallow!

You're one very talented elephant. I wish my sister were half as good as you!
Hey, Hans! I heard that!

You aren't jealous of a baby elephant, are you?

Aren't you supposed to support me?

Okay... You did well!
But, what can I say, Team Marshmallow is just much much cooler!

What kind of brother ARE you?

Loser pays
for ice cream!
Jordan is
so good.
At this rate, I'll be broke
from buying you ice cream!

LITTLE LEAGUE CHAMP
Kahawaii Multicultural Sc
Too bad she can't join us at Regionals. It's so unfair! Just because she's in a wheelchair.

That's the official rule, and we all know it. Even Jordan.
Yeah...

It's been two years... She understands why she can only play with us at practice.

Still, it's hard to see her look so sad when we assign the team roster each year.
KMS 18
LITTLE LEAGUE CHAMPIONS

Marshmallow! Let's go!

We're going to Anita's for ice cream! Lynn is TREATING us!

She said it's ALL-YOU-CAN-EAT pineapple Cold Whip today!
WHAT?! I didn't say that!
Listen, you two, just one Cold Whip per person!

WHIP
ANITA'S
COLD WHIP

AYAM GORENG

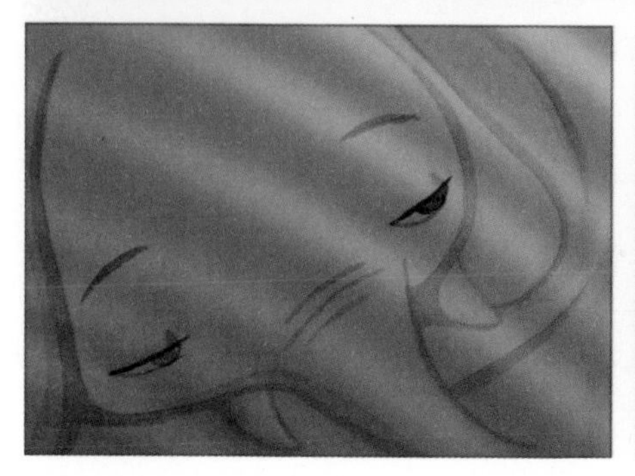

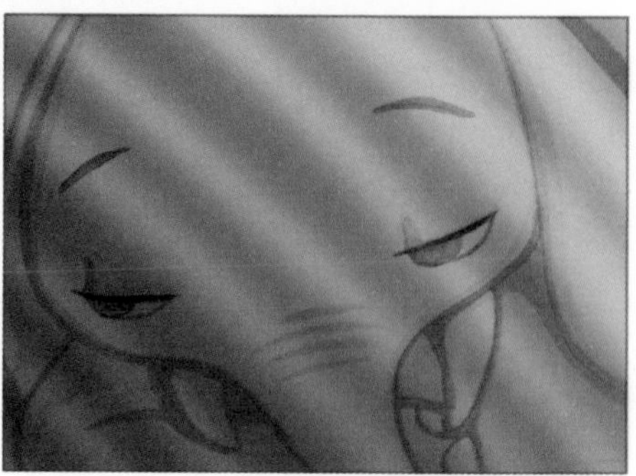

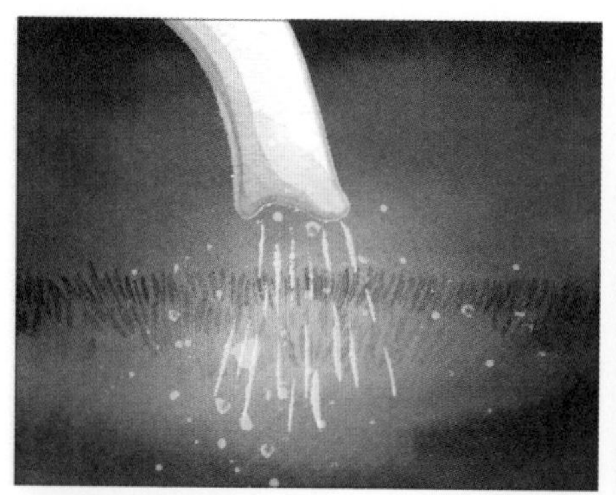

Marshmallow?

What is it?

WOW...

What's Onde Dikit giggling about this early in the morning?

SPLASH
SPLASH

This is easier than expected!

Ma?
Look!

It's wonderful to see her swimming. It's been so long.

You ARE invited to
JORDAN's
SURPRISE B-DAY PARTY!!
SUNDAY
oct 8
1 pm @
JORDAN's
HOUSE
P.S. Don't tell JORDAN!!
GLUE

NAMAAZ

Two dozen each of ayam goreng and pisang goreng, please.

Sign here, please. It'll be about thirty minutes.
SIGN
Okay, we'll pick it up later.

Meanwhile, at home

Now let's go get some mango and durian.

Why are we getting so much food?

It's for Nenek's sewing club meetup at the temple.
I thought there were only four or five old ladies in her sewing club. That's a lot of food for just them!

Never under-estimate the superpowers of little old ladies.

Haven't you seen those eating contests on TV? Most of the time the winners are scrawny!

I'm always curious where they put all that food?

Dad, are you implying Nenek and her friends eat like pigs?

You, Monyet Kecil! That's not what I mean! Don't put your stinky foot in my mouth!

What I mean is that Nenek and her friends are very healthy, good eaters. Nothing more!
Heh! Backpedaling.

Back at home
Halo, Marshmallow!

Halo, Mrs. Winarta.
Welcome, everyone.

Is there anything we can help with?
Jordan'll be back soon. If you can help set the rest of the table, that would be great!

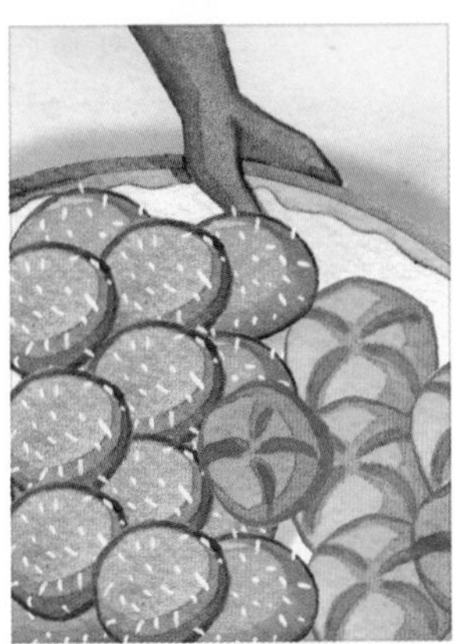

Coach, Taman. Thank you for coming. Oh, little Buana has grown so much.

Think Nenek would let us eat a little bit of the ayam goreng?

We're home!

Mom? Nenek? Marshmallow?

Where is everybody?

SURPRISE!!!
HAPPY BIRTHDAY!!

SQUEAL!!

Happy Birthday, Monyet Kecil!

SMILE!

What're you doing?
Blowing up J's b-day gift!

You know they've got a pump, right?

What?
How do you think I inflated my donut?

Wait for me!
Anyone up for a game?
Count me in!
Me too!

I'll play!

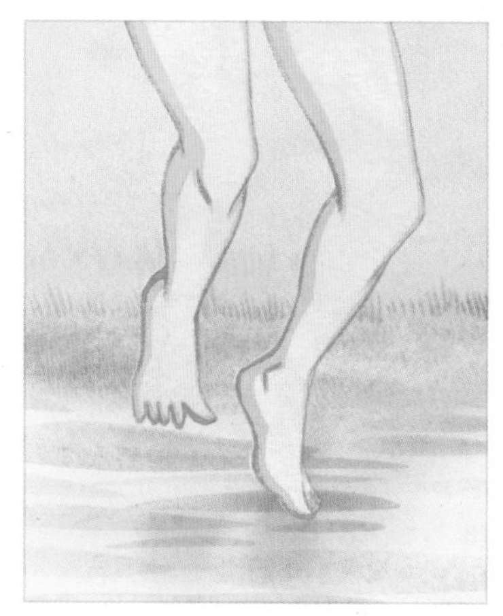

What are the rules?

NO RULES!
Whoever scores most wins!

All right!

Game on!

COACH?!
Could you be our referee?

Okay!

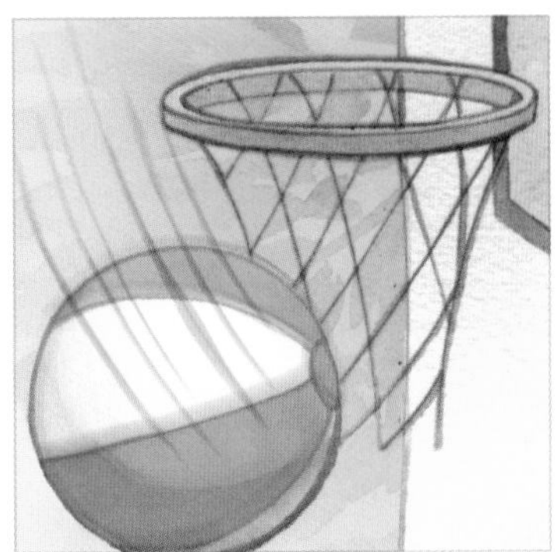

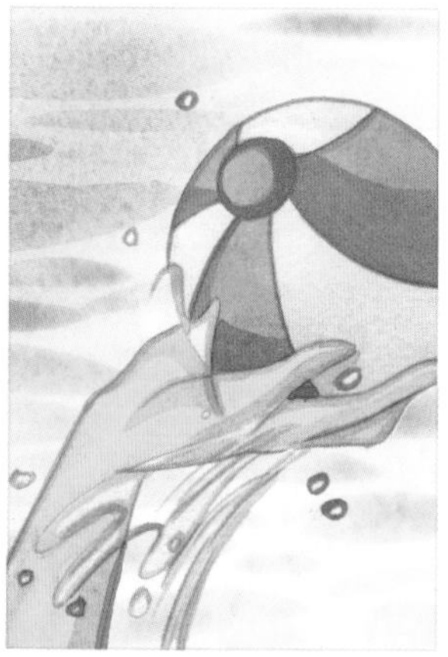

FOUL!!
That doesn't count!
NEW RULE!
Offense can't shoot from immediately under the hoop!
Second attempt must be at least three meters back!

WHAT?!

They've got a point! Otherwise, we'll just hang around the hoop.

FWEET

ROUND TWO!

Coach is the referee. You can't boss us around!

Terima kasih!
Yeah, right! He's not even watching the game.

Round Two!
Ready? Go!
PENALTY!
Alyssa!
THE BALL!

Oops...
GO, JORDAN, GO!

BLOCK HER!

Don't let her pass the ball to Lynn!

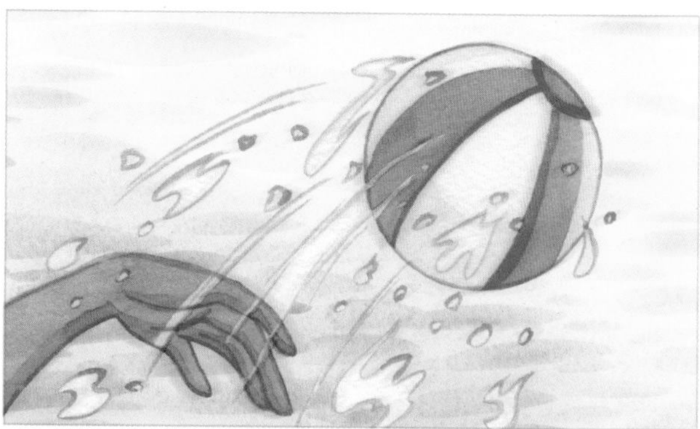

That's incredible!
Team Jordan just scored.
One to zero!
That's amazing!
How long has
Jordan been
swimming again?
A few weeks...
She swims as much
as when she used to
train for triathlons.

She should see about joining the school water polo team. I bet with training she could compete.
Compete...with the school water polo team, huh?

Jordan scores again! Two to zero!
What? How?

DANG! She just swished that from more than half the length of the pool! She can channel Steph Curry in the water too?

WOW! It's
a Marshmallow
team jersey!
23

We had it designed specially for you.

This is from the whole team. You'll always be our captain, no matter what!

Marshmallow, thank you.

Today when I was in the pool, playing with the gang, it felt like I was running with them, like we used to.

Best birthday ever!

Have you played water polo before?

No, but I can't wait to learn the game.

Great! Let me introduce you to the team.
FWEET

Everyone, this is Jordan.

She's in a wheelchair?

Jordan is joining the team today. Please make her feel welcome.
11
5
5

Kemala, Jordan is new to water polo. I want you to help her get to know the team and our training routine.

Jordan, Kemala is the team captain.

Feel free to reach out to her if you need help with anything.

Aren't you on the basketball team?

Er...yeah, I'm on the basketball team.

Since Amisha graduated last spring, we haven't been able to find anyone good enough to recruit for competition.

Jordan comes highly recommended by Coach Prayogo. She'll be a perfect fit for our team.
Is she gonna be able to compete?
What?
Can she even swim?

So you don't even know how to play water polo?
What's coach thinking?
NO, not yet.

Don't worry. Water polo is similar to soccer and basketball. You'll pick it up in no time.

Why don't you join our practice today?

I would love to.

Let's take a break while Jordan is getting ready.

It may take some time for the kids to warm up to Jordan.
Does she know this is a leg sport?

It's unfortunate that in a small town like ours, there aren't any disabled leagues. This will give Jordan a chance to be an active athlete in a school team.

We're going to start with some dry ball handling practice.

Five laps of freestyle, five laps backstroke.
Try to keep the ball above and in front of your head.

Afterward, five laps of the ball-in-hand technique that you learned last week.

Not the ball-in-hand...
My arms were sore for days.

Kemala, I want you to lead the drills.
1

Jordan, since today is your first practice, I'll be working with you individually.
11
3

Let's have you start with a few laps, so we can analyze how to tailor your training to your strengths.
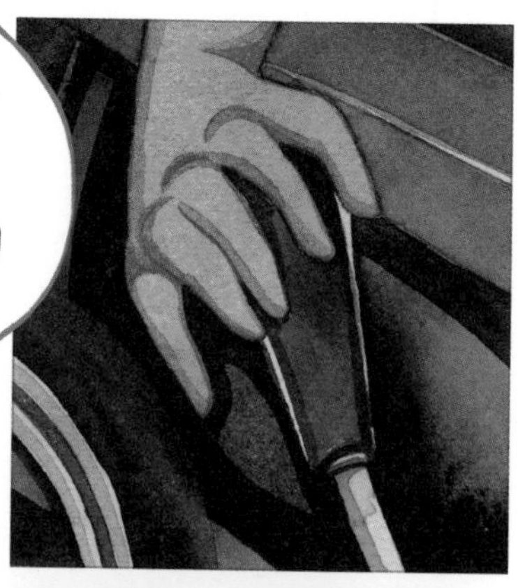
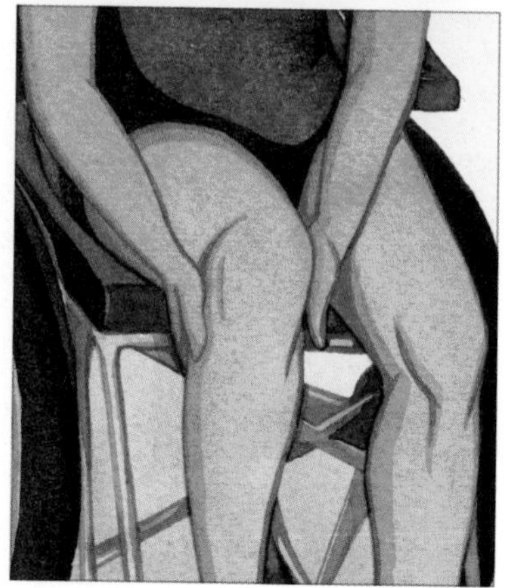

Meanwhile...
Today we're going to start prepping for Regionals.

Lynn, you'll be the new team captain.

What about Jordan?

Some of you already know that, unfortunately, official rules won't let Jordan compete at Regionals.

KMS

She's still part
of the team, right?

Jordan IS on
the team and
she can come to
the games with
us, but she
can't compete.

Then why isn't
she here today?

The water polo
team needed a new
player. After seeing Jordan
swim at her birthday party,
I recommended her to Coach
Ahmed. She's joining them
for practice today.

WHAT?!
You already knew that, right?!

Back at the pool
Well, at least she can swim.
YEAH, RIGHT! A sea slug could swim faster than that!
12
5

Try to rotate your shoulders more. It'll help you to gain speed.

You've got great upper-body strength! However, you'll need to learn how to use your upper-body muscles differently to build more speed.

Hey, Wayan!
5
3

Huh?

5

This means war!
5
HEY, you two!
The competition is right
around the corner.

Can you TRY to take practice seriously?!

With a sea slug joining the team, our chances of passing the first round are slim as it is.

URGH!

Let's wrap it up!

Coach, can I stay and practice a little longer?

Of course you can. Just don't overdo it.

The competition is months away!! Why is Kemala freaking out already?!
12

It's getting late.

We've gotta go.
But we ALWAYS walk home together.

Mom just texted again. Ojichan is getting cranky.

Make sure J gets home safe.

Halo, Jordan.
Halo...

You worked hard on your first day!
Terima kasih!
I thought everyone left already.
No, well... I stuck around to work on my art assignment.

You're working on your art homework at the pool?
I need to draw people swimming, so I drew you just now.

Can I see your drawing?

Sure, but the drawings are still very rough.

WOW! These are amazing!
SKETCH

You're very good!

Thanks!

By the way, I don't know your name.
I'm Paola.

ZZZ
Marshmallow!

Thanks for waiting!
You've got an ELEPHANT?!

This is Marshmallow!
You're adorable!

This is my place.
No way. I'm just around the corner!

Recent wildfires and drought are taking a painful toll on Ketut's farming regions...

Jordan, do you want to go to school together tomorrow?
Sure!

You'll love this manga! It's funny.
Hey, J!

Hey, everyone!

We've been looking everywhere for you!

Let me know how you like the book. See you later!
Chips?

Who was that?
That's Paola from water polo.
We miss you at practice!
I miss you too!

Our first game is Friday. We're playing Negara Academy at home.
I heard.
This will be Marshmallow's first game ever!

And your first game as captain. I wouldn't miss it!

Promise?

Pinky promise!

You know, this will be our very first game in middle school too!

Basketball game day
I'm so nervous.
I don't think I can eat...

If you don't
eat that, I will.

Go for it!

There's a
pregame party
at three thirty.
You should
come!

I wouldn't call it a
party. It's more like an
unofficial parent/teacher
thingy to talk about
expectations, goals,
performance...
Boring stuff.

I've got water polo practice today. I don't think I can make it to the party, but I'll come to the game for sure!

Sorry, emergency bathroom run!

We'd better check on her!

WELCOME To KAHAWAii

You're well prepared. Don't worry about the score. Just do your best and have fun out there!
KMS 18
KMS 11
KMS 15
KM 17

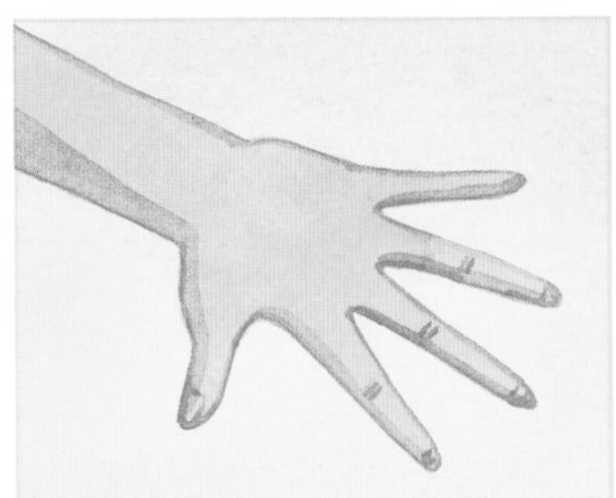

GO, Kahawaii, GO!

KMS 6
KMS 21
KMS 15
KMS 11
RESERVED

RESERVED

RESERVED

Go KAHAWAii
Negara Rock
KMS 5
KMS 11
KMS 15
5
10

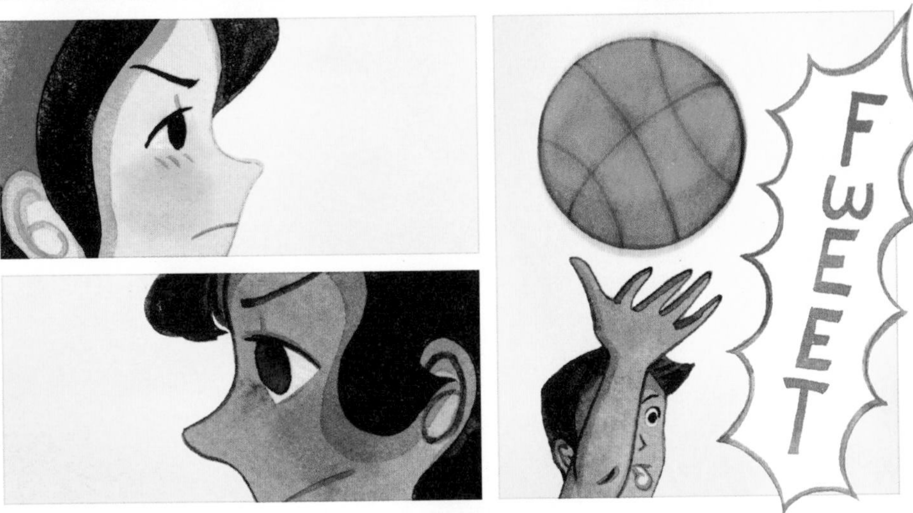
FWEET

Meanwhile...
You need to stay and practice your offense some more.
But the basketball game is starting!

Our tournament isn't that far away, but YOU are far from ready!

AMANDA! WAYAN! You two aren't going anywhere either!

WHY?

You both showed up late and you were goofing around half the time.

Not fair! Our class ran late!
TWENTY LAPS! The sooner you finish, the sooner you can go.
Jordan, I'll work with you on some offensive and defensive tactics.

Stroke.

Chop cross.

This technique allows you to fence off your defender to free yourself.
Now you try.

Pretend I'm your opponent. *GO*!

Not bad.
Let's go through it a few more times.

11
12
1
10
2
9
3
8
4
7
6
5

It's five already. How many laps have we done?
I lost count. Let's just go!

Jordan! If you want to catch the last bit of the game, you'd better go now!
Don't think they can hear you.

I didn't say you could go yet!

Back at the basketball tournament

KMS
18
KMS
15
KMS
21

RESERVED

Still at the pool

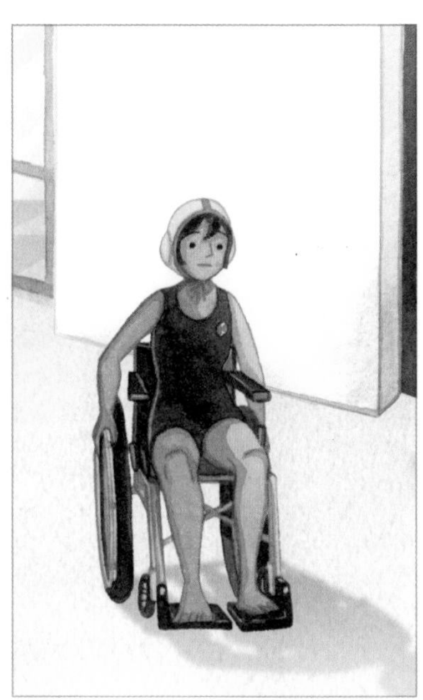

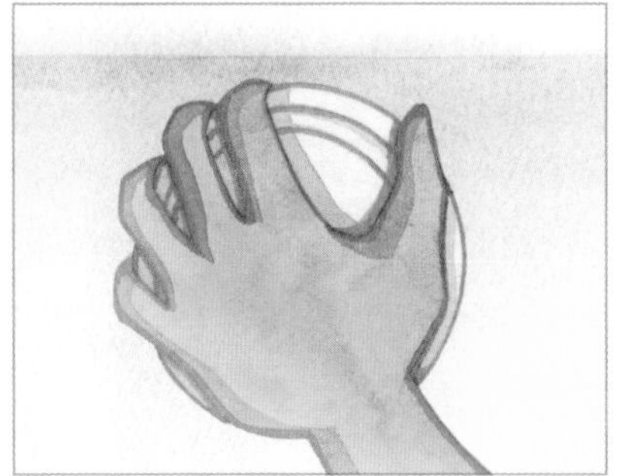

Welcome To Kahawaii !!
Paola...

Jordan, what happened? How come you're all wet?

Kemala made me stay for extra practice. I rushed here as soon as I could...

Let's get you dried off!

KMS
15
KMS
11
KMS
5

KMS

Look! We're in the school paper!

Halo, everyone!

Congrats...

They've been ignoring me for weeks.

I was hoping Lynn would've forgiven me before winter break, but...

Spring semester
EVERY DROP
COUNT

PICNIC
DANCE

KMS
KMS

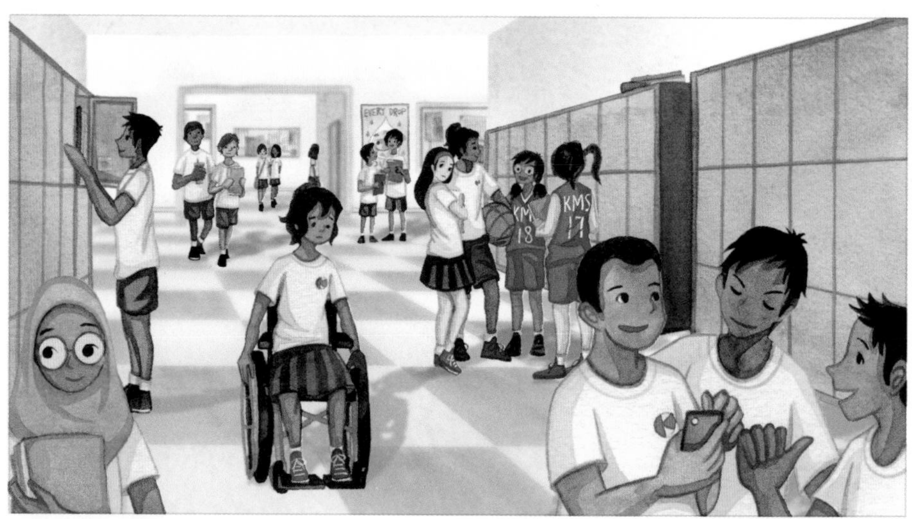
EVERY DROP
KMS 18
KMS 17

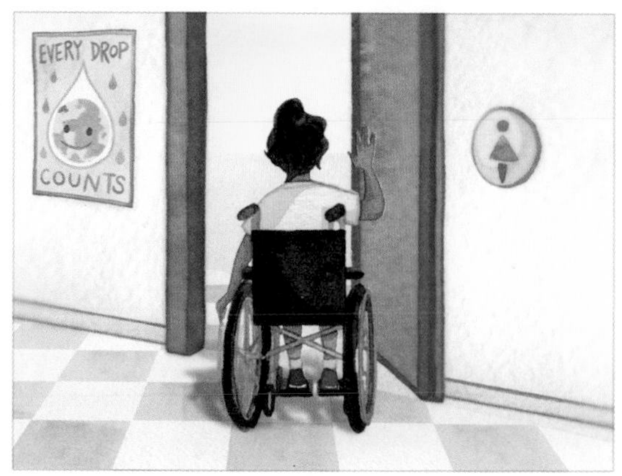
EVERY DROP
COUNTS

Kemala!

Kemala, what's bothering you?
I'm afraid I'll be disqualified for the sports scholarship.

Our farm isn't doing well because of the drought. I need the scholarship to pay for tuition.
You get good grades. I'm sure you'll be okay.

NO! I won't be okay if we lose in the first round.
?

We're missing a player, and not everyone takes practice seriously.
But we're NOT missing a player.

COME ON, Sarah! Jordan is useless! She barely swims.

She's okay. She's actually getting better.

OKAY IS NOT GOOD ENOUGH! The game is next month.

If I lose my scholarship, I won't be able to go to school here next year.
We'll work hard to prep for the game.

SAVE WATER SAVE LIFE

Three weeks until the game

Marshmallow, what's up?

How's J doing?
Has she been doing extra training on her own all this time?

No wonder I've barely seen her this semester.

Where did you come from? You are LATE!

Have you talked to J lately?
NO!

I don't know what happened between you two, but you should check in with her sometime.

WHY? She broke her PINKY PROMISE and ditched me for her water polo friends.

J's having a very hard time right now. You two've been BFFs since kindergarten. Just check on her, okay?
Humph!

Lynn?

Hey, J...

Are you here alone? Where's your team?
They're done with practice already.

Why are you still here, then?

I need to do extra work to prepare for the competition. I don't want to drag the team down.

Why do you think you'll drag them down?

Cuz I can't swim fast enough, and I still have so much to learn.

I'm sorry.

I missed your first game. I had to stay behind for extra practice that day.
7

I miss you...
I'm sorry.
I should've been
here for you.
I miss you too.

I'll come by to
help you practice
so you're ready
for the game.
Terima
kasih.

Water polo game day
WAIT!

Wait for us!

Huh?

Coach Ahmed, we got permission from Coach Prayogo to come with you.
You must be Dea and Alyssa. You're right on time. Hop on!

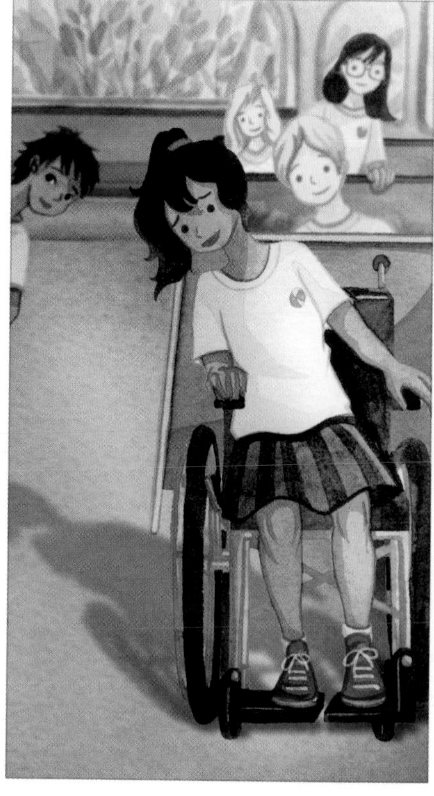

Hey, J!
Alyssa! Dea! What're you doing here?
Lynn called us to help you out. She's taking Marshmallow to the game.

What?! How?
Don't know... She was kinda mysterious about it.

Lollipop?
Terima kasih.

Lollipop?
I don't like sweets.
I'm Alyssa. What's your name?
I'm Amanda.
Wayan.

Paola, want a lollipop?
JUICE

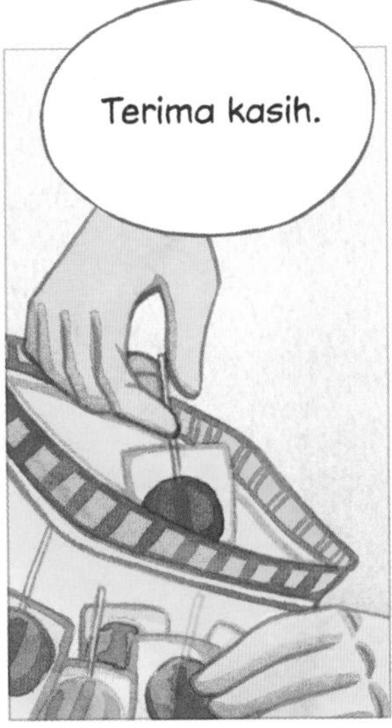
Terima kasih.

Please pass the candy to the back!

Terima kasih! I'm Sarah and this is Lee.

I'm Alyssa. I can't wait to see you play. I've never been to a water polo game before! So exciting!
JUICE

What's your name?
Kemala.
Are you nervous about the game? You look a bit tense.

I'm fine.

You sure you don't want some candy? It'll help you relax.

Fine.

No one can ever melt the ice queen... She's COOL!
That's the spirit!

Save your strength for the game. I'll be your muscles today.
Terima kasih banyak.

Where is it?
Do you want some water?
EVERY DROP

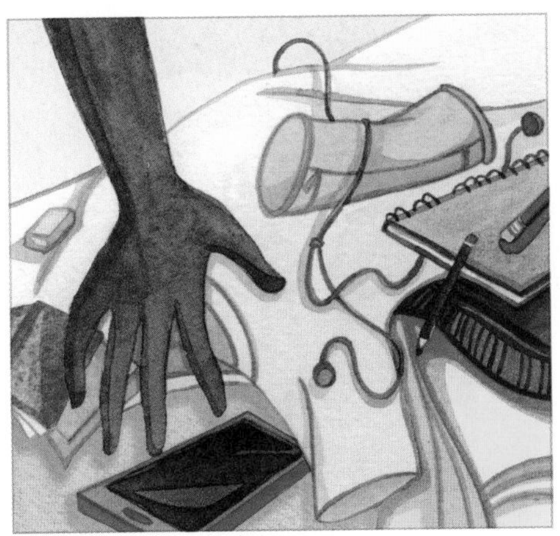

SHAMPOO

Has anyone seen my cap?

Did you pack it?
Did you check all the pockets in your bag?

AWWW...
What should
I do???

Isn't there a cap
hanging on the
locker door?

3

Wayan, are
you number 3?
3

YAY! That's
mine!

It's time!

Why am I nervous.
I'm not even playing!
I know, right?

GO, KAHAWAII, GO!

OMG, is that a baby elephant?

Here is your stop. I'll be cheering for you!
Good luck!
Terima kasih, everyone.

WELCOME TO
CANGGU PUBLIC SCHOOL
HOME
GUEST
0
0

Are they even middle schoolers? They look like high school kids.

That info doesn't help!
Let's be positive! Height probably doesn't matter as much in water sports.
Actually, we've got a good team too. We have J. AND I read online...
#1
...Kemala is quite amazing. She got into Kahawaii through a prestigious water polo scholarship.
6

FwEET

CANGGU ROCKS!

Lestair is FAST! Kemala can't even get close enough to block her.

Ndari,
catch!

JORDAN!
OH NO!

HOME
1

GUEST
0

This is not a good start...

Don't panic! We've got time to catch up. Make sure there's enough defense at the goal.

Sarah, catch!

I'm blocked!

Sarah's stuck...

FWEET

What's going on? Why did J get a penalty?

She gets a twenty-second penalty for pushing that girl underwater.

Don't get
down on yourself.
This is your first game.
Mistakes happen.

That girl's
totally faking it! How
could J push her down?
She's so much bigger
than J.

10
1
Oh NO! Canggu
scores again...

Jordan, you can go back now. Good luck!

GO, Jordan, GO!

Amanda, catch!

Amanda,
behind you!

Go, Amanda!
You can do it!

Kemala!

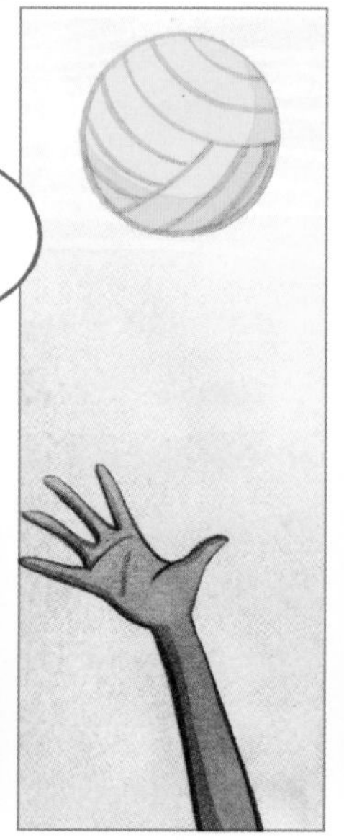

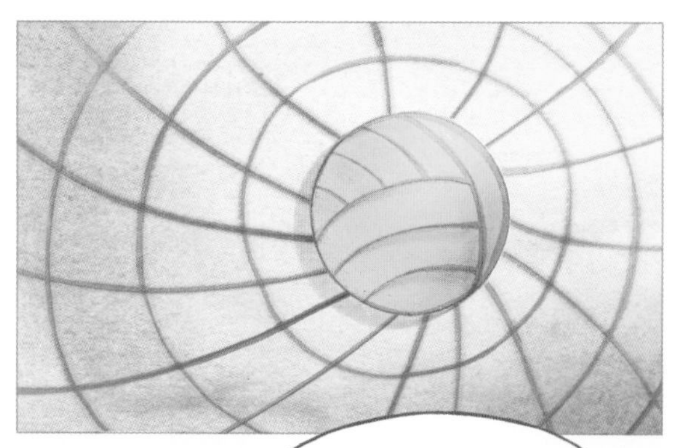

GO, KAHAWAII, GO!
Kemala ROCKS!

7

Second period begins!

10

PAOLA! Give the ball to Amanda!
10

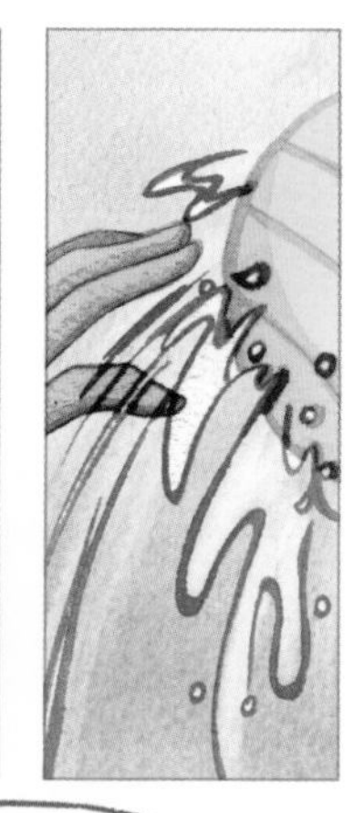

How come she won't pass the ball to J?

J is totally open. There are no defenders near her.

7
5

Sarah!
7
I think they're worried, after her earlier mistake.

She needs a chance, though.

12

YAY! Now we're even!

Finally, I can relax a bit.

We need to break the tie. Let's focus our defense on Kemala.

FWEET

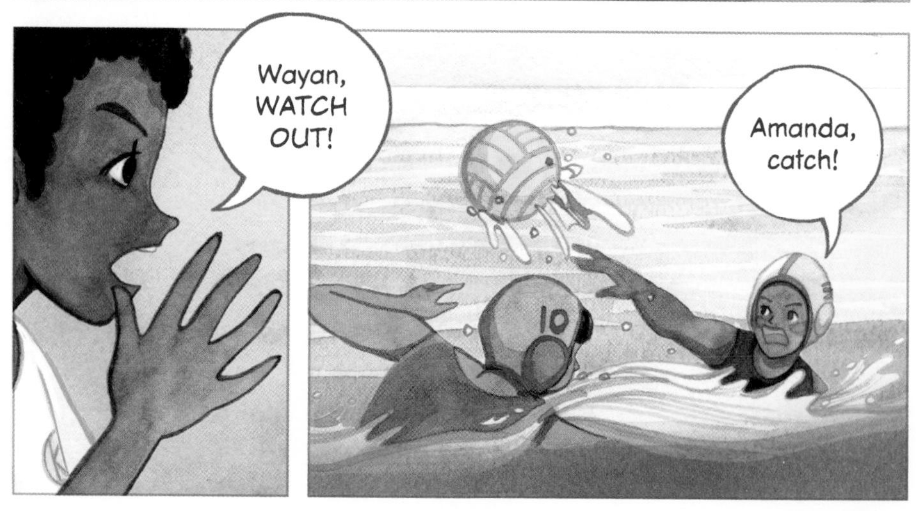
Wayan,
WATCH
OUT!
Amanda,
catch!
10

That was close...

AMANDA, GO GO GO!!

KEMALA!

She's completely surrounded.

KEMALA, PASS THE BALL TO JORDAN!

KEMALA! PASS THE BALL TO JORDAN!!!!
Time's running out! Give the ball to Jordan!
#1

1

TRUST US! JORDAN CAN SCORE IN TEN SECONDS!!!

There's no way your team can score in ten seconds.

WHAT?!

NO WAY!

YES!

Three Seconds

Two Seconds

SCORE!

YAY!! WE WON!

That shot was unbelievable for a middle schooler.

She is especially gifted.

...
She scored from the twenty-meter line. How's that possible?!

You're AMAZING!!!
10

She uses a wheelchair?

If only we knew you could shoot like that, we wouldn't have had to train so hard.

That was so awesome!

Terima kasih, Sarah.

You should have seen the looks on the other team's faces when you scored!

Jordan.

Glad to have you on the team.

Kemala...
Terima kasih.

Kahawaii vs.
Bangung School
Kahawaii vs.
Surabaya International
Kahawaii vs.
Diakonia Public
School

Kahawaii vs.
Tangerang Academy
Kahawaii vs.
Pelangi School
District Champions
Kahawaii Water Polo Team

One month later
Kahawaii is one of the strongest contenders for the National Finals. The team is led by Kemala Nalapraya...

She is a familiar face to fans of middle school water polo.
Hey, girls!
LOOK! We're FEATURED on Lesser Sunda Aquatic vlog!
That's HUGE!

What put Kahawaii on our radar is their new member Jordan Winarta.

Her precision in long-distance shooting makes her the second-highest individual scorer in this season's tournament.

J, you're famous!

Now that Jordan is in the spotlight, she'll be under a lot of pressure.

The highest-scoring player is still Kemala Nalapraya...

Kemala! That's a NICE shot of you!

Regional Finals will be very competitive.

You worry too much. With you and Jordan on the team, we're UNBEATABLE!!
LISTEN!
With the two highest-ranking players on the same team, we predict that Kahawaii will advance to Nationals.

We need to defeat Bali Academy to qualify. Don't forget they won the national title last year.

Kemala has a point.

Both Jordan and Kemala will be heavily defended in the upcoming competition.

It'll be a lot harder for them to score.

Haven't you noticed that Kemala's scoring rate dropped in the last couple competitions?

Yup!

You'll need a new strategy. I've been analyzing all your competitions. Here's a plan.

J, you need to improve your short-distance acceleration speed to break away from the opponent's defense.

That should give you the crucial extra second to get the ball.

Start
Stop
Reset
00:05.42

Kemala, when you're trapped inside five meters...

...It's okay to let your opponent get the ball.

WHAT?!

Wayan, you're great at defense. You'll be responsible for stealing the ball back.

Pass the ball to another teammate.

Whoever catches the ball can pass it back to Kemala.

Kemala, you'll be J's decoy. As soon as you've got the ball, the opponents'll block you.

This will weaken their defense on Jordan.

Now you'll pass the ball to Jordan.

J, you may still have at least one person blocking you.

You need to push your speed to the limit to catch the ball...

...and shoot!

That's a very risky plan.

It's wild, but it should get you out of some sticky situations.

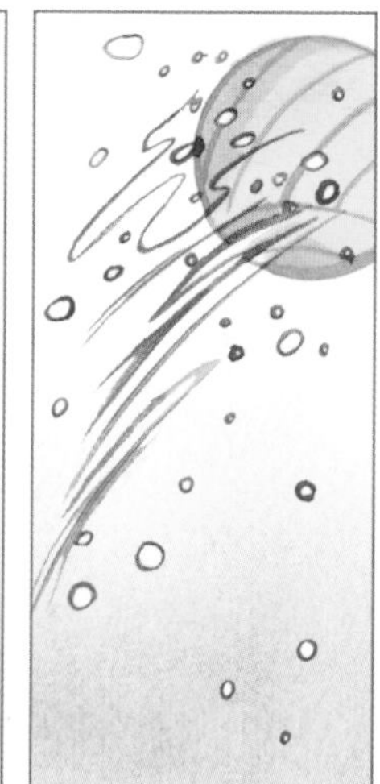

Kahawaii wins!

Oh my god!
Dea, your crazy
plan worked!

KAHAWAII WATER POLO
Lesser Sunda Regional
Middle School Water Polo Champions

KAHAWAII WATER POLO

Congratulations, everyone. I am very proud of you.

HAWAII WATER POLO

Jordan!

Marshmallow is here. Let's go!

KAHAWAII WATER PO

Coming!

ANITA
Today's Special
Banana
Pineapple
Tamarind

Last week of school
Is everyone going to Anita's later?
Yup.
I'm not going to miss out on FREE TOPPING DAY!

Marshmallow will be meeting us at the gate.

Let's meet after assembly.

First, I would like to congratulate Kahawaii Middle School Water Polo team for winning the Regional Finals.

Our middle school basketball team also had a successful year.

They won third place at the Lesser Sunda Semifinals.

While we have much to celebrate, we must not forget we are currently living through the most severe drought in the history of our island.

Many of our friends in the agricultural community are suffering from devastating financial losses due to the drought.

In order to reduce water usage at Kahawaii, the school will be shutting down all aquatic facilities this summer and the following school year, unless the situation improves.

The Kahawaii School Board and the Parents Association have set up a donation site...
...to help raise funds to support students and families in need during this climate crisis.
I would like to wish you all a restful summer vacation and I look forward to welcoming you back next academic year.

We won Regionals. But if the school stops supporting water sports, I'll probably lose my scholarship. If that happens, I won't be able to come back next year.

SCHOOL

Dea, you're quiet today. Are you all right?

I was going to tell you guys later. I'll be transferring to another school next year.

Why? Not you too.

My dad got laid off from the farm last month. He's looking for a new job on other islands.

Didn't your dad work at Batukaru? They're one of the biggest farms.

Doesn't matter!
The drought's killing
all the crops.

Let's go to Anita's.
We should still celebrate the
end of the school year.

I'm going to
miss everyone.

It has been
a fun year.

Where is Marshmallow?

He was here a moment ago.

Maybe he went to the pool? Or the basketball court?

Don't worry, J. We'll spread out and find Marshmallow. You stay here, in case he comes back.

Nenek, is Marshmallow at home?
He left to go to the school a while ago.

Marshmallow?

Marshmallow?

I'm going to check the classroom. You go check the lunchroom.
Okay!

Marshmallow?

Marshmallow?

We looked everywhere, but no luck.

We looked all over the campus. We can't find him either.

Wait... I think I know where he went.

Marshmallow?

Marshmallow?

Are you sad because you overheard our conversation at school?

The...the drought is my fault...

You... can talk?

Actually, I'm not an elephant... I'm a rain cloud.
What do you mean?

I'm the cause of the drought.

The drought is no one's fault. Nobody can control the weather.

I'm your regional rain cloud. Since I came here, there hasn't been any rain.
I don't understand...

I live in the sky. The day you found me was the day I ran away from home. I tripped and fell to Earth.

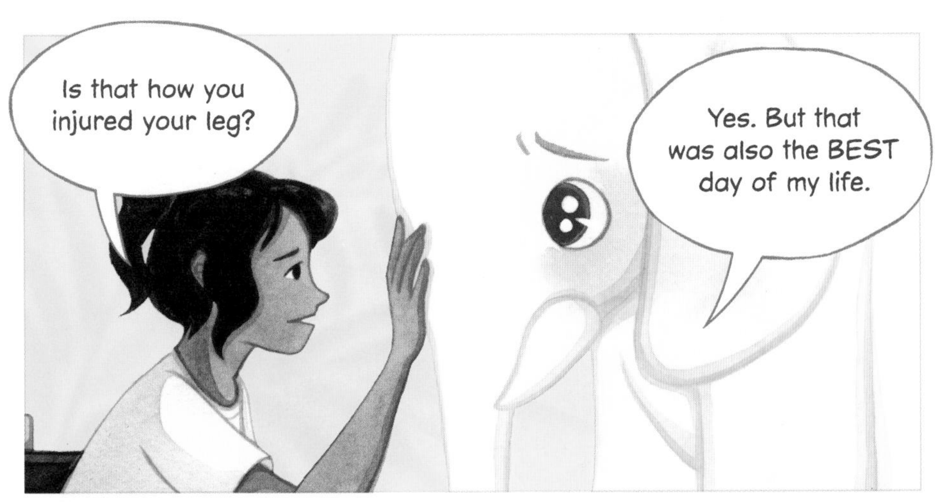
Is that how you injured your leg?
Yes. But that was also the BEST day of my life.

You took me home. Nenek spoiled me.

Then I met all of you. I've never had so many friends.

Back home, I didn't really have any friends. Everyone made fun of me...

...and teased me, and called me "crybaby," because I'm a rain cloud.
That's horrible.

Thunder liked picking on me. When I cried, everyone laughed at me. I HATED being a rain cloud, so I ran away.

Poor Marshmallow!
We love you, Marshmallow.

I love you too. But I have to go home.

If you like it here, you could stay with us forever.

I can't bear to see everyone hurting because of me. The longer I stay, the worse the drought will get. I have to go home and fix everything.
Please stay just a little longer.

Sorry we're late. We stopped by Anita's on our way here.

We got your favorite pineapple Cold Whip with extra coconut topping!

Anita asked us to give you a hug. She'll miss you too.
ANitA

Will you be lonely when you go back?

I won't be lonely, because I have all of you now.

Tell us if Thunder or any of the other stupid weather spirits give you a hard time.

Yes! Ping us in our dreams, so we can send them stink-bomb offerings.

You'll always be our team mascot.

It won't be the same without you cheering for us.

Even though we can't hang out like before, I'll cheer for you from up there.

Promise?

Pinky promise.

You may want to try another promise. Jordan's pinky promise is jinxed.

I blame Kemala for messing up my pinky promise.
How is it my fault? You used to swim like a sea slug.

Yeah? A sea slug who saved your butt a few times.

Marshmallow. Terima kasih for teaching our sea slug how to swim.

We'll miss you, Marshmallow.
We'll never forget you!

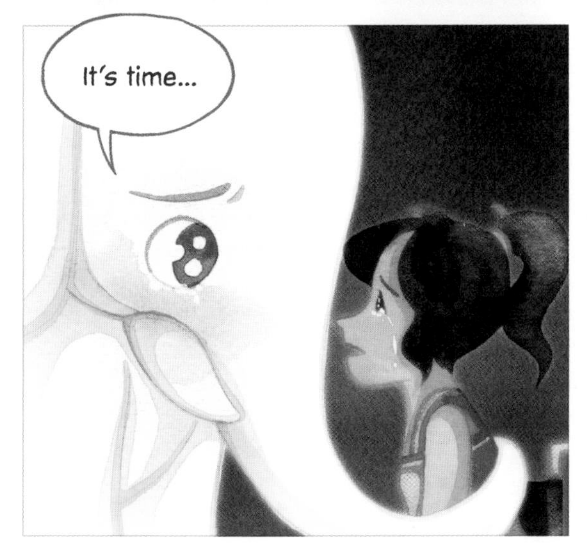
It's time...

You'll always be my best friend.

Terima kasih for taking care of me.

Goodbye, Jordan.

Take care, Marshmallow.

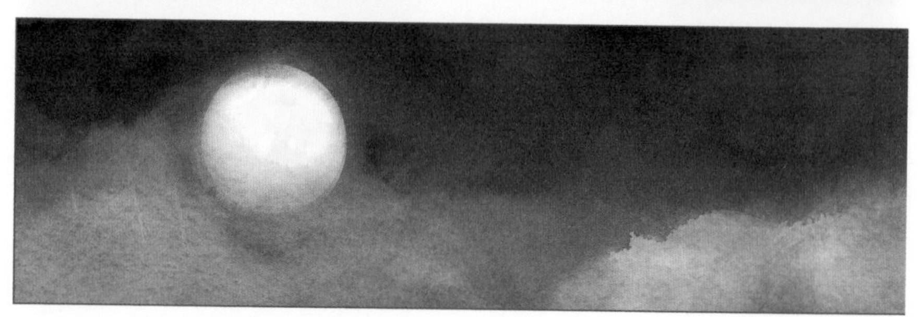

A year later
This year's National Middle School Water Polo title goes to Kahawaii Multicultural School.
INDONESIA MIDDLE SCHOOL
WATER POLO NATIONAL CHAMPIONSHIP

Marshmallow!

AUTHOR'S NOTE

There are many stories about kids embarking on wild adventures due to unexpected events. They get into mischief, perhaps acquire magical powers, defeat monsters, fight treacherous villains, and maybe even save the world. Yet most of these children are able-bodied.

While writing this book, I did a lot of research into the everyday life and sporting activities of paraplegic children and athletes. I wanted to depict Jordan and her wheelchair use with respect and accuracy. However, like any fantasy fiction, I took creative liberties, giving our heroine a natural athletic talent closer to a young Olympian's. While Jordan still needs to work hard to learn a new sport, her learning curve, stamina, and reflexes are above average.

Marshmallow & Jordan is a fantasy story set in Indonesia. Jordan is a mortal girl with a physical disability, but she is confident and determined. She does not let her use of a wheelchair define her. She rescues a deity-in-training, survives middle school, and achieves extraordinary success despite few people believing in her. Marshmallow is her opposite. His image is loosely inspired by Airavata, a Hindu white elephant god who can knit clouds and helps Indra create rain. Marshmallow inherits Airavata's supernatural power of controlling rainfall. However, as a deity-in-training, he is insecure and timid.

Jordan gives Marshmallow unconditional friendship, while Marshmallow broadens Jordan's horizons and helps her see her potential. Though this is fantasy fiction, I hope that every reader can see themselves in this story.

Visual development painting

Visual development painting

MARSHMALLOW'S MINI DICTIONARY

- Ayam goreng — Indonesian fried chicken
- Durian — A large tropical fruit with a strong odor and thorn-covered rind, which is considered the "King of Fruits" in Southeast Asia
- *Ganesh* — The Lord of Obstacles, the elephant-headed god, is one of the most worshipped Hindu deities.
- Halo — Indonesian for "Hello"
- Monyet Kecil — Jordan's dad affectionately teases Jordan, calling her "Monyet Kecil." *Monyet* means "Monkey." *Kecil* means "Little."
- Nenek — Indonesian for "Grandmother"
- *Ojichan* — Japanese for "Grandfather"
- Pisang goreng — Indonesian fried banana
- Terima kasih — Indonesian for "Thank you"
- Terima kasih banyak — Indonesian for "Thank you very much"

Marshmallow's Recommendation

Lemper ayam is a savory snack made of glutinous rice filled with seasoned shredded chicken, wrapped in banana leaf.

Jordan's Recommendation

Onde-onde is a cute little traditional Southeast Asian dessert made out of sweet glutinous rice with the center filled with palm sugar. Nenek gives Jordan the nickname "Onde Dikit" because onde-onde is Jordan's favorite dessert. The funny way Jordan's family addresses her is inspired by the quirky habit of nicknaming in my family.

Lynn's Recommendation

Jus alpukat is Lynn's favorite drink, and it's an authentic Indonesian smoothie. These sweet, rich, and popular avocado-chocolate beverages are made with avocado, milk, condensed milk, and chocolate. It's the perfect post-practice refresher.

Nenek's Recommendations

From left to right:

- Sago gula melaka is a Malaysian pudding made from sago, pandan leaves, palm sugar syrup, and coconut milk. This version is wrapped in a banana leaf.

- Bolu kukus is a soft and fluffy Indonesian sponge cake with a texture simliar to chiffon cake.

- Jian dui are fried sesame balls made from glutinous rice flour with a red bean paste filling. This pastry originated in China back in the Tang Dynasty. Today, this snack is popular throughout Indonesia.

Visual development painting

MR. AL-SAMARRAI'S FUN FACTS ABOUT INDONESIA

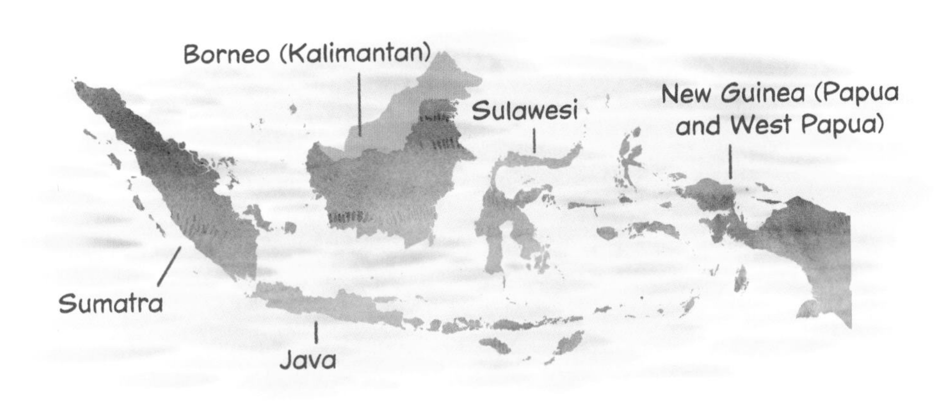

Indonesia is a country in Southeast Asia and Oceania, between the Indian Ocean and Pacific Ocean. It consists of 17,508 islands, of which around 6,000 are inhabited.

The largest islands are Sumatra, Java, Borneo (divided with Brunei and Malaysia), Sulawesi, and New Guinea (divided with Papua New Guinea).

Indonesia is the world's largest island country and the fourteenth largest country by land area.

Indonesia lies along the equator. Its climate tends to be relatively even year-round: It's tropical with wet, hot, humid weather. However, the primary variable of Indonesia's climate is not temperature, but rainfall.

Instead of four seasons, Indonesia has just two: hot and dry, and the rainy monsoon.

Agriculture is a key component of the Indonesian economy. One of the world's largest agricultural nations, Indonesia exports a wide variety of tropical crops, including palm oil; natural rubber; cocoa; coffee; tea; cassava; rice; and tropical spices like pepper, nutmeg, vanilla, cinnamon, cloves, ginger, and cardamom.

However, in recent years, Indonesia has faced more severe drought than in the past. The harsh dry season makes the country more vulnerable to forest and peatland fires. The shifting climate significantly impacts the Indonesian Archipelago due to scarcity of clean drinking water and declining supply of irrigation water. This leads to crop failure.

Climate change is a global issue. Each of us can help reduce global warming by reducing our carbon footprint.

- Reduce, reuse, and recycle.
- Save electricity and water.
- Car rides are convenient, but walking or biking both save energy and are good exercise as well.
- Plant a tree or bee- and butterfly-friendly gardens.
- Be a science champion and raise awareness.

Small actions make BIG differences!

Visual development painting

Character design concept art

J! Awww... My sarong shrank in the laundry. I've got nothing to wear to the festival!
I have a pink sarong that would look cute on you. Let me look.
Terima kasih!
Are you sure the sarong shrunk? Maybe you're getting chubby!

MOMMMM! HANS IS PICKING ON ME!!!

What is this?
Marshmallow?
MARSHMALLOW'S Diary
Dearest Jordan,
I wanted to tell you my real identity for a long time, but I never found the right time or courage. So I decided to write down my story.

Acknowledgments

Thanks, Marietta, my amazing agent! Without her inspiration, this book would not exist at all! When I first wrote a story about a white elephant, it was a historical-fantasy picture book. Marietta suggested that I contemporize and expand the idea into a graphic novel! Marietta, your support and wisdom throughout this long creative journey has been invaluable.

Maria, I can't ask for a better editor than you, and I'm lucky you're also my good friend. Developing a graphic novel is a long, lonely process. I can't thank Maria enough for riding this "roller coaster" with me. Thank you for lifting me when I tripped and celebrating each milestone with me. You made this journey fun, even on days when we burned the midnight oil and worked in a hotel room on a holiday.

Anita! YES!! She IS the same Anita who owns Cold Whip Ice Cream in the book. But in real life, Anita is an art gallery owner. Anita and Maria were the first people with whom I shared the concept of *Marshmallow & Jordan*. Whenever I get exciting ideas or I freak out due to a work crisis, Anita generously offers her love or a shoulder to cry on and always cheers me up!

Last but not least: thank you, Calista, at First Second, for believing in my story and acquiring *Marshmallow & Jordan*.

✿ Terima kasih, TEAM MARSHMALLOW!! ✿

To my Nenek, Mom, Dad, and Piglet.

:01
First Second

Published by First Second
First Second is an imprint of Roaring Brook Press,
a division of Holtzbrinck Publishing Holdings Limited Partnership
120 Broadway, New York, NY 10271
firstsecondbooks.com
mackids.com

Library of Congress Control Number: 2021906595

First edition, 2021
Edited by Maria Ludwig and Steve Foxe
Cover design by Kirk Benshoff
Interior book design by Sunny Lee
Special thanks to Alex Blaszczuk and Jacquelyn Ryan

Sketched and cleaned up in Photoshop.
Hand-painted with watercolor on paper and digitally composited in Photoshop.

Printed in China by RR Donnelley Asia Printing Solutions Ltd., Dongguan City, Guangdong Province

ISBN 978-1-250-30061-4 (paperback)
1 3 5 7 9 10 8 6 4 2

ISBN 978-1-250-30060-7 (hardcover)
1 3 5 7 9 10 8 6 4 2